Whittington
and his cat

Written and illustrated by Anne & Ken McKie

Published by
GRANDREAMS LIMITED,
Jadwin House, 205/211 Kentish Town Road,
London NW5 2JU

Printed in Belgium

ISBN 0 86227 327 7

Long long ago in a tiny village in England, lived a very poor boy called Dick Whittington. He was all alone in the world since his mother and father had died. The village folk were very kind to Dick. They gave him food and the few clothes he had. But they were poor as well and had very little themselves. Dick was a good boy, and helped them by doing work in return for their kindness. This way Dick learned to do all manner of jobs really well. He could bake bread, weave cloth, repair houses — and even mend wheels on carts.

One morning, Dick saw a few of the village people gossiping together on the village green. As he had nothing better to do he stopped to listen. They were talking about a great city many miles away, where the streets were paved with gold.

"If I wasn't so old," said one man, "I would go there myself!"

"If I had a good horse," moaned another, "I would ride to London this very day!"

"So that is where the streets are paved with gold," whispered Dick, very excited. "I will go there at once and see for myself."

So the next morning, as soon as the first rays of sun were glinting through the trees, Dick crept out of his cottage and tiptoed through the sleeping village.

He walked all morning over the hills and valleys until he came to a wide dusty track used by waggons and horses. "So this is the way to London town," Dick said out loud. A jolly man on a cart shouted back: "It's a long walk, lad! Over a hundred miles." Poor Dick's face fell. The man laughed. "Climb up on the cart, boy! You can drive while I sleep — and see you don't tip us in to the ditch!"

The journey to London took many days and Dick was grateful for the ride. At last one evening, as Dick drove the cart to the top of a hill, he spied the city of London far in the distance. So many houses — so many streets — and so many church towers. Dick couldn't wait to reach the gates. Soon, they crossed London Bridge and the jolly man with the cart went his own way. As for Dick, he rushed off to find if the streets really were paved with gold.

He searched and searched until it was dark, but of course he found none. Then very tired and very hungry, he fell asleep in someone's doorway.

What a shock Dick had the following morning! Instead of waking up to the sound of birds singing, he woke up to the noise of the city. People scurrying about arguing and yelling. Some carrying all manner of goods and shouting their wares in the street. Waggons rattling by — horses — dogs — even sheep — but most of all, lots of people.

Dick just sat and stared. All at once a door opened behind him. A great big hand reached out and grabbed him by the ear. ''Get out of this doorway, you good-for-nothing boy,'' yelled the angriest woman Dick had ever seen. ''This is the house of Mr. Fitzwarren,'' she screamed at Dick, and promptly threw him into the muddy street. ''He's due back any minute. And I don't want him to find you lying on his doorstep.''

Luckily for Dick, Mr. Fitzwarren was just crossing the street. He was a kind man and was sorry for the poor boy. "Come, come, Cook," he said to the angry-looking woman. "I'm sure you can find work for this lad in your kitchen. But first get him some food and fresh clothes."

So that is how Dick Whittington came to be kitchen boy in the house of a wealthy merchant named Mr. Fitzwarren.

How hard the bad-tempered cook made Dick work. All the day long he scoured the pots and scrubbed the black sooty pans. At night the cook made him sleep in an attic full of rats and mice. All night long they scampered around in the straw of Dick's bed. Some nights he got no sleep at all.

It was Dick's duty every morning to walk to the market to fetch food for the cook to prepare. Most of the stalls sold chickens and ducks or fruit and vegetables. There was one stall that sold animals and birds. And in one of the boxes was a cat.

This gave Dick an idea. ''Will you sell your cat for one penny?'' the boy asked the stall holder (for one penny was all Dick had in the world). ''That's just right,'' the woman said, as she grabbed the penny eagerly. So now Dick was the proud owner of a cat. ''I shall call you Tibs,'' the boy decided. ''I know we shall become the best of friends.''

That very night Tibs ran ahead up to Dick's attic room. She killed every rat and mouse before Dick reached the top of the stairs. Soon, Tibs had got rid of every rat and mouse in the house. Alice (Mr. Fitzwarren's daughter) came down to the kitchen to thank Dick. She was delighted because she hated rats.

It so happened that Mr. Fitzwarren owned several big ships. They sailed from the port of London carrying goods to faraway lands. Each time one of his ships was ready to sail, the merchant asked all his servants if they had any goods to sell in a distant land, and he would bring them back lots of money.

Everyone sent something — except Dick, who owned nothing at all. "Send your cat!" suggested Alice. "I am sailing with my father and I will look after her." Poor Dick felt he had to say yes to please Alice.

After the ship sailed away, the Fitzwarren's house seemed very empty. Dick missed Alice and he was really lonely without Tibs. All too soon his attic became full of rats and mice. Even the cook was more cruel to him than usual.

Dick was so unhappy he made plans to run away. He slipped out of the house very early and tried to find his way to London Bridge. As he passed Bow church, the bells began to ring. He hurried on, but the bells seemed to call him back.

He stopped to listen, and they seemed to say.

"Turn again, Whittington,
Lord Mayor of London."

"I can't run away now," cried Dick. "I will turn again and I will become Lord Mayor of London." And with that, he ran all the way back to the merchant's house. Not even the cook noticed he had been missing.

Faraway over the sea, Mr. Fitzwarren's ship was in great trouble. The voyage had lasted weeks and weeks with no sight of land. Tibs the cat had made herself very useful and killed hundreds of mice and rats that swarmed all over the ship. Sad to say, the weather was getting much worse every day. The ship was pitching and rolling and enormous waves washed the deck. Not one of the crew was brave enough to climb the rigging to look for land. "This is the worst storm I have ever known," said Mr. Fitzwarren in despair. Alice began to cry. "If we don't reach land soon, we shall all be drowned!"

Before anyone could stop Tibs, she climbed up to the top of the mast to look around. The ship was rolling in the gale, but Tibs hung on tight with her claws. By some miracle she managed to get back safely on deck. "Did you see land, Tibs?" demanded Mr. Fitzwarren. The cat nodded. "Was it far away?" cried Alice, and Tibs shook her head.

Knowing that land was ahead gave the sailors new hope. They all worked hard with the sails and the steering and gradually made it to the shore.

The people there had never seen a great sailing ship before. They made the Fitzwarrens and all the ship's crew very welcome, and took everyone straight to the Sultan's palace. The Sultan who ruled this land was very rich. His palace walls were studded with precious gems, and his tables and chairs were made of gold. He ordered a great feast to be prepared, and everyone from the ship was made welcome.

When all were seated round the golden table, the Sultan clapped his hands for the servants to carry in the food. Row upon row of them came forward with heavy covered dishes made of gold. At a signal from the Sultan, the servants leaned forward and removed the covers. What a wonderful sight! Mouth-watering meats and luscious fruits, they could hardly wait to begin.

Then it happened! Rats! Huge, fat, black rats! Shrieking and squealing, they swarmed all over the table. Soon, every scrap of food had vanished.

The Sultan wrung his hands in despair. "This happens at every meal. My kingdom is full of rats. My poor people have nothing left to eat." He leaned across the golden table to Mr. Fitzwarren and Alice. "Look," he cried angrily, as he lifted up his foot. "They even chew our leather slippers." And he wriggled his toe through a big hole. "I would give half the treasure I own, to rid this land of rats!"

Alice smiled at her father. The crew from the ship smiled at each other. For on Alice's knee, out of sight under the table, was Tibs the cat.

"Let go of the cat, Alice," suggested her father. Quick as lightning Tibs shot from beneath the table and pounced on the nearest rat. She moved so fast she soon killed all the rats that swarmed across the floor. Some of them escaped and ran up the curtains, but Tibs was too quick for them. In no time at all she had killed every rat in the palace.

Once every rat was dead, Tibs jumped in the Sultan's lap to be stroked. What a scene followed! The Sultan yelled and fell off his throne. All the royal family screamed, and some of the servants fainted. You see, none of them had ever seen a cat before. They thought Tibs was going to kill them too.

Alice picked up the cat and began to stroke her. "You see how gentle she is," said Alice, burying her nose in the cat's soft fur. Tibs purred with pleasure.

It took ages for the Sultan and his family to come anywhere near the cat. But after a while they were brave enough to tickle her tummy.

"Please don't ever leave us," the Sultan begged Tibs. By now the cat had killed every rat in the kingdom.

"We must set sail for home now," said Mr. Fitzwarren. "We will return with lots of cats on our next voyage. So never again will you be plagued by rats!"

The Sultan was so grateful he filled the ship with as much treasure as it could carry. To Tibs the long journey back home seemed endless. She had missed Dick so much.

What rejoicing there was, when at last the ship sailed up the River Thames and into London. What tales Alice and her father had to tell.

When at last all was told, Mr. Fitzwarren ordered the sailors to bring the Sultan's treasure from the ship. It was so great it filled the room.

''Come forward, Dick Whittington,'' ordered the merchant. ''It was because of your wonderful cat that we were given all this treasure. By rights, Dick, all this belongs to you.''

Of course the rest is history.

Dick became a rich man. After a while he married Alice Fitzwarren and lived happily ever after.

Just as Bow bells foretold, he did become Lord Mayor of London — not once — not twice — but three times.

His name is part of history and remembered all over the world to this day.....

"Turn again, Whittington,
Lord Mayor of London."